Surrounded by Safety

MARYANN TOLSON

ISBN   978-1-953821-72-0 Ebook
ISBN   978-1-953821-71-3 Paperback

The EC Publishing LLC books may be ordered
through booksellers or by contacting:

EC Publishing LLC
116 South Magnolia Ave.
Suite 3, Unit F
Ocala, FL 34471, USA
Direct Line: +1 (352) 644-6538
Fax: +1 (800) 483-1813
http://www.ecpublishingllc.com/

Ordering Information:
Quantity sales. Special discounts are available on quantity purchases by corporations, associations, and others. For
details, contact the publisher at the address above.

Printed in the United States of America

TABLE OF CONTENTS

Acknowledgments v
Why I Wrote this Book..vii

PART 1
Retired Sergeant Mark Miller...2
Spiritual Mom and Spiritual Son 5
You Will Always be a Policeman To Me 7
Retired Sergeant Mark Miller and His Daughter Lisa.............9

PART 2
KIND THINGS ABOUT POLICE.....................................11
Policeman Bought A Car Seat..12
Christmas Gift's from Police Officer Woman at the Door 14
A Kind Policeman Gave Me A Ride Halfway Home 16
Surrounded by Safety 18
Kind Policeman on the Curb...21
5 Police Men Praising Jesus...23
Police Officer Getting His Praise on at Church.....................25
Massive Mob Overwhelms School's Favorite Police Officer 27
Well Informed Police Lady 29
Kind Police Officer from HY-VEE..31
The Local Police Encouraged a Little Boys Dreams................33

PART 3
Retired Sergeant Robert..36
Bible Scripture On What to Think On...................................44
Prayer for Police and Fire Fighters 45

ACKNOWLEDGMENTS

Thank You, God, for creating me.

Thank You, Jesus, for dying on the cross for me. Thank You, Holy Spirit, for leading me into truth.

To my mother, Patrica, and my father, Jerry—thank you for helping to create me.

Thank you to my spiritual momma, Talya, who prophesied that there were many books within me.

Thank you to Retired Sergeant Robert for sharing his life story in my book.

Thanks to my brother in the Lord, Retired Sergeant Mark Miller, for allowing me to write about him and his K9s.

Thanks to my former pastor, Randy Waterman (now in heaven), who always encouraged me to keep writing.

And to all the men and women in blue who have made a difference in my life and countless others—thank you.

WHY I WROTE THIS BOOK

God inspired my heart one day to write about the positive experiences I have had, heard about, and witnessed involving police officers over the years.

Anyone can point out the bad things a person does, but God has called me to focus on the good. Since I have been going to church with Retired Sergeant Mark Miller for many years, he has always been a great influence in my life and a true example of what it means to be a police officer. I believe this is because he is a born-again believer, and Jesus has helped him throughout the years to be a role model for both the police department and the world.

This book is dedicated to honoring him and all those who faithfully serve as true and upright men and women in blue—as well as the firefighters who put their lives on the line.

I appreciate you all, and always remember—Jesus loves you.

PART 1

RETIRED SERGEANT MARK MILLER

Retired Sergeant Mark Miller is an amazing man of God. I first met him in 1999 at Church of Compassion when Cowboys for Christ joined us, and we sang together in the choir.

He is an incredible singer and guitar player who loves Jesus with all his heart. He has loved singing since he was a child and began playing the guitar in high school.

Another amazing thing about Retired Sergeant Mark Miller is that when I first wrote about him in my book, he had been a police sergeant for two years. Throughout his career, he had two

K9 partners, both named Emir. For 13 of his years on the police force, he also served as a K9 handler.

Mark has four wonderful children from his first marriage—two beautiful daughters and two handsome sons, all of whom are now grown.

In 2016, Retired Sergeant Mark Miller married a very beautiful young lady named Amy, who is a detective. Amy has a radiant smile that lights up any room and a personality to match. When they got married, I wrote them a wedding poem, and their hearts were so touched by it.

Retired Sergeant Mark Miller and Detective Amy, you are both such a blessing.

Thank you for all you do for our church and this world.

Dear God,

Thank You for bringing Retired Sergeant Miller and Detective Amy to Celebration. I love them very much, but I know You love them even more.

In Jesus's name, Amen.

And thank you for the beautiful thank-you card—it truly touched my heart.

Thank you, Retired Sergeant Mark Miller, for 30 years of dedicated service on the police force.

SPIRITUAL MOM AND SPIRITUAL SON

Retired Sergeant Mark Miller and Miss Shirley adopted each other as mother and son.

She's beautiful, and he's the handsome one. They're like two peas in a pod, always sticking together—their relationship is one of true love.

Whenever they are together, the smiles on their faces reflect God's love.

True love has no color, and it shines brightly through these two.

Spiritual mom and spiritual son, your relationship inspires everyone around you.

Keep on loving each other as you do, and always remember—Jesus loves both of you.

YOU WILL ALWAYS BE A POLICEMAN TO ME

You will always be a policeman to me even though you are not a policeman anymore the memory of you being a policeman I will always adore every time that I see you a smile comes on my face you are one of the kind brothers in the Lord in our church place actually we all feel safe whenever we are around you because for years we were surrounded by safety by you I'm sure many people in the community feel the same way too and your partners Emir one and two we're very memorable too thanks again for many great years of service and thanks for sharing your great talents on the praise team too you are a blessing to everyone around you and always remember that Jesus loves you and I love you too

RETIRED SERGEANT MARK MILLER AND HIS DAUGHTER LISA

Retired Sergeant Mark Miller and his daughter Lisa shared a beautiful bond when she was a child. She looked so lovely, and I must say, the man in blue looked mighty fine.

She was so proud to hold her daddy's hand, and he was just as proud to hold hers.

He has always been a wonderful father—everyone around him knows this to be true.

Retired Sergeant Mark Miller, you are an example to me and to our church family.

You have held a special place in my heart for the 30-plus years that I have known you.

Keep on loving your children as you do, as well as everyone who comes into your life.

And always remember—Jesus loves you.

PART 2

KIND THINGS ABOUT POLICE

POLICEMAN BOUGHT A CAR SEAT

You bought a car seat for a little girl to help keep her safe. Her father couldn't afford one because he had too much on his plate, but he was deeply touched by your kindness and generosity.

Your compassionate heart is surely a gift from the Father above.

To the policeman who bought a car seat for a little girl—keep on being kind and protecting us as you do.

And always remember—Jesus loves you.

babytrend
Roll over image to zoom in

CHRISTMAS GIFT'S FROM POLICE OFFICER WOMAN AT THE DOOR

One day, my husband heard a knock at the door. When he opened it, he was amazed—standing before him was a policewoman with a warm smile.

She held presents in her hands, hoping to give them to a child in need. But our kids were grown and gone, so she had to find another home. That was okay, though, because many children lived in the apartments nearby.

Thank you, policewoman, for spreading Christmas cheer. It was such a kind and thoughtful thing to do.

God bless you! I was so inspired by your kindness that I wrote this poem for my book.

Policewoman, keep on loving children as you do, and always remember—Jesus loves you.

A KIND POLICEMAN GAVE ME A RIDE HALFWAY HOME

When I was 15, I had gone through a very traumatic time with a couple of guys that I had known for some years. I tried to take it to court, but because of lack of evidence, I couldn't find my shoes that got lost at the place they took me and tried to rape me. My case got thrown out of court. So, since I grew up with the guys, a lot of places that I went to, they were there too. So, one night I had a ride to a party. And when they saw me, they were coming at me like they wanted to kill me! They started screaming at me to get out!

I was scared so I left. I had no idea where I was because it was dark outside. So, I started walking and crying. All of the sudden I saw a police car. I was desperate for help. so, I ran over to the police and asked him if he could give me a ride. I don't believe that they can normally give someone a ride but because he saw that I was desperate, and I told him my situation he took me as far as he could. I recognized where I was at by then I was so thankful for that ride I was 15 and now by the grace of God I made it to 60 and I'm still thankful for that kind policeman giving me a ride that day if it wasn't for that kind policeman giving me a ride it could have been fatal.

AUTO REPAIR
& BODY SHOP
212-643-6770
HIGHWAY PATROL
COURTESY
PROFESSIONALISM
RESPECT
NYPD
POLICE
NYPD
POLICE
824 10

SURROUNDED BY SAFETY

I thought I heard firecrackers when I woke up one day. Then I thought, *This couldn't be—it's only May.*

As I lay back down to sleep a little more, I heard more pops. *That sounds like a gun for sure,* I thought.

I called the office, and the manager said she heard gunshots too. I told her I was getting ready for work, and she said, *I called the police. I would stay inside if I were you.* She was concerned for my safety—and so was I.

A little later, I looked out the window, and what did I see? The police taking someone out in handcuffs. A peace came over me—I felt surrounded by safety.

There were many police cars and officers in blue, doing what they are trained and paid to do—keeping us safe.

I thanked them for their service as my face lit up with a smile. I told them I was writing a book of poems and that one would be dedicated to them inside.

Surrounded by safety, I appreciate the good work you do. Thank you for risking your lives for me and countless others too.

I know the media shows a lot of bad things some police officers have done, but they haven't met kind and caring officers like you.

Thanks again for all that you do, and always remember—Jesus loves you.

My name is Maryann Tolson, with Songs of Inspiration. I am here to bring healing to the nation.

KIND POLICEMAN ON THE CURB

I saw a video one day that really touched my heart.

A policeman was sitting on the curb, talking to little kids—letting them know that police are their friends. He gave them popcorn, helped those who needed assistance opening their bags, and even ate with them.

Some of the kids told the policeman they loved him, and he said he loved them too.

Kind policeman, that moment truly touched my heart. When I saw what you did, I knew that God in heaven saw it too.

Keep on sharing love and kindness with children as you do, and always remember—Jesus loves you.

5 POLICE MEN PRAISING JESUS

I turned on my Facebook page, and what did I see?

Five policemen praising Jesus—oh, how it encouraged me!

They were thanking Jesus in a song,
With smiles on their faces, grateful for His amazing grace.

I could see the love of Jesus shining through them as they praised Him.

Five policemen, keep on praising Jesus as you do,
And always remember—Jesus loves you.

24

POLICE OFFICER GETTING HIS PRAISE ON AT CHURCH

As I was scrolling through YouTube one night, I saw something that touched my heart in a special way.

A praise service was happening at a church, and to my surprise, a police officer was there—getting his praise on!

He was dancing so fast, praising his Heavenly Father with joy. I got so excited that I watched it over and over again.

He had no shame—he was doing his **praise thing!**

MASSIVE MOB OVERWHELMS SCHOOL'S FAVORITE POLICE OFFICER

School's Favorite Police Officer, I Congratulate You!

You're amazing—this is true.

As I watched this video, my heart filled with joy. You touched the lives of so many people, and I could see that their hearts were full of joy too.

You treat others the way you want to be treated. You not only keep them safe, but you also genuinely care about them. You impact their hearts and lives in such a way that they want to honor you.

It must be the love of Jesus inside you that makes you care so deeply for people of all ages.

You are a great example of a faithful, caring officer.

Keep making a difference in all that you do, and always remember—
Jesus loves you.

WELL INFORMED POLICE LADY

We appreciate you coming to our Women of Worth meeting. We learned so much from you and gained valuable awareness.

Personally, I now pay more attention to my surroundings because of what I learned from you. Thank you for taking time out of your busy schedule to help us stay informed about the challenges in our world today.

We are also grateful for you sharing your personal experiences and the things you have been through.

Once again, we appreciate you, and always remember—**Jesus Christ loves you.**

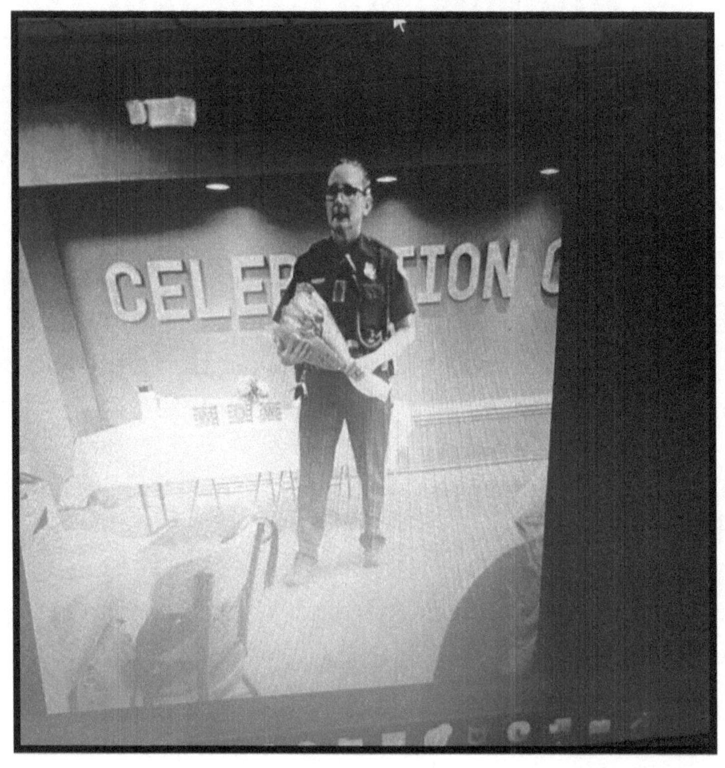

CELEBRATION

KIND POLICE OFFICER FROM HY-VEE

Thank you for always being kind to me whenever I came to Hy-Vee through the years. I also appreciate your kindness toward my son and the way you continued to ask about him even after he no longer worked there.

Whenever I came to the store, I always felt safe around you. It was clear that you truly enjoyed the job you did.

Kind police officer, thank you for being part of my book, and thank you for being a true officer in blue.

Keep up the great work, and always remember—**Jesus loves you.**

THE LOCAL POLICE ENCOURAGED A LITTLE BOYS DREAMS

When the local police department learned that a little boy dreamed of becoming a police officer, they gave him the adventure of a lifetime.

An officer greeted him by name, shook his hand, and said, "How are you?" He also told the boy he was looking sharp in the little police shirt they had given him. Then, the officer asked, "Do you want to go for a ride with us?"

The boy eagerly replied, "Yes! I want to catch some bad guys!"

The officers went above and beyond—taking him to his favorite lunch spot, showing him all the police vehicles, and, most importantly, making sure he had a whole lot of fun. It was a day he would remember and smile about for years to come.

They even dressed him up like a real police officer, complete with a hat, handcuffs, a badge, and a whistle.

PART 3

RETIRED SERGEANT ROBERT

I want to start by thanking God, my Creator and Redeemer. Through Him, all glory and grace are given, and He has granted me the opportunities I have had in this life. I also thank Him for His steadfastness and grace, especially during the low points in my life, as well as the times when I walked away from Him and chose my own path instead of following Him. Through it all, He never forsakes us. He is always there to pick up the broken pieces of our lives when we make mistakes. Every experience in my life is part of His design and will. Any achievements I have had are by His grace and for His glory, not my own.

I would also be remiss if I did not thank the author for taking the time to consider me and my story for this publication. It was an honor to reflect on the past three decades of my service to the greatest country in the world, serving in the most powerful military the world has ever seen, and sharing my small piece of that history. The last of those three decades was spent serving my local community as a police officer, which was just as rewarding, though in a very different way.

My name is Robert Haxton, and I was born and raised in Iowa.

I graduated from Waukee High School in 1991, where I excelled in football and basketball. I later attended and graduated from

Waldorf College in Forest City, Iowa, where I also played basketball during both years as a student.

In 1993, after graduating from Waldorf, I enlisted in the U.S. Army and attended basic training at Fort Sill, Oklahoma, where I trained as a field artillery meteorologist. Immediately following my training, I attended Basic Airborne School at Fort Benning, Georgia, before arriving at my first duty station: the 319th Headquarters and Headquarters Battery Division Artillery (HHB DIVARTY), 82nd Airborne Division, at Fort Bragg, North Carolina. For nearly 13 years, I was on jump status as a U.S. paratrooper and later a jumpmaster.

In 1996, I joined the ranks of the Noncommissioned Officer (NCO) Corps, was promoted to Sergeant, and took command of a team of three troopers within my section at HHB DIVARTY. During this time, I met my oldest son's mother, Pengia, and we were married in 1994. My son, Jonathan, was born in May 1996.

In 1997, I reclassified my Military Occupational Specialty (MOS) to Military Police (MP) and attended MP basic training at Fort McClellan, Alabama. From there, I was reassigned to the 82nd Airborne Division's 82nd Military Police Company at Fort Bragg, NC. The company's primary mission was to provide combat support to the three infantry brigades of the 82nd Airborne Division:

- **1st Brigade**: 504th Parachute Infantry Regiment (PIR)
- **2nd Brigade**: 325th PIR
- **3rd Brigade**: 505th PIR

At that time, the 82nd MP Company had four platoons, each consisting of approximately 21 military police officers. Each platoon had three squads, with each squad supporting a battalion within the brigade. I was assigned to 4th Platoon, responsible for securing Division Headquarters during a division-wide operation—the first of its kind since World War II.

After about a year, I was reassigned to the 55th Military Police Company in the **Republic of Korea**, where I spent a year on a hardship tour, away from my family. This was extremely difficult for both Pengia and me, as she had to raise our young son alone while I was overseas. Being apart for so long was just as hard on me as it was on her. This assignment, along with later deployments, was one of the major reasons for our eventual divorce in 2002.

After my tour in Korea, I returned to Fort Bragg and rejoined the 82nd MP Company, this time in 3rd Platoon as a team leader. Soon after, I was promoted to squad leader in 2nd Platoon, where I led **3rd Squad**, supporting 3rd Battalion, 325th PIR. I remained there for the next two to three years.

In January 2001, my squad deployed to **Kosovo** in support of **Operation Joint Guardian** under Kosovo Forces (KFOR) for approximately seven months. While there, we supported operations for 1st Battalion, 325th PIR. Our duties included:

- Conducting **route reconnaissance and security missions** in the Vitina sector
- **Interdiction operations** along the Macedonia-Kosovo border, targeting rebels smuggling weapons, narcotics, and personnel
- **Detaining Albanian rebels** and transporting them to Task Force Falcon Headquarters at Camp Bondsteel

During this deployment, I was promoted to **Staff Sergeant** in May 2001.

I returned home in July 2001 and transferred back to 4ᵗʰ Platoon, where I served until I left the **82ⁿᵈ Airborne Division** in September 2002. That same month, my wife and I finalized our divorce due to irreconcilable differences.

After leaving the **82ⁿᵈ Airborne Division**, I was assigned to the **Joint Readiness Training Center (JRTC) Operations Group (Airborne)** at **Fort Polk, Louisiana**, where I served as a **Military Police Observer Controller**. In this role, I provided feedback and facilitated **After Action Reviews (AARs)** for maneuver units conducting military training exercises. I served there until 2005, gaining valuable experience in battle staff operations and mission tracking at the battalion and brigade levels. This assignment significantly enhanced my abilities as an NCO.

In 2005, I was assigned to **A Company, 701ˢᵗ MP Battalion** at **Fort Leonard Wood, Missouri**, where I served as a **Military Police Instructor**. While I appreciated the **Ozark Mountain region**, I did not enjoy this assignment. I found the MP schoolhouse to be overly concerned with statistics rather than quality training and soldier proficiency. Additionally, being in a **non-deployable** unit frustrated me. Despite this, I was promoted to **Sergeant First Class** during my time there.

In the **fall of 2007**, I requested and was reassigned to the **57ᵗʰ Military Police Company, 728ᵗʰ MP Battalion** at **Schofield Barracks, Hawaii**, where I took command of an MP platoon of about **40 soldiers**. My platoon had recently returned from a **15-month deployment to Iraq**, and leadership challenges were prevalent. Thankfully, my **platoon leader, Jon Combs**, was one of the best officers I had ever served with, making my role as **platoon sergeant** much easier.

In **August 2008,** I volunteered for an **individual augmentee deployment to Afghanistan** in support of **Operation Enduring Freedom (OEF).** I was deployed to **Camp Eggers, Kabul,** where I served as a **Force Interrogation Sergeant** for the Afghan Border Police (ABP) and Afghan Counter-Narcotics units.

During this deployment, I participated in **poppy eradication operations** in **RC-South** (Kandahar and Spin Boldak), working alongside U.S. **Special Operations Forces (SOF)** and international coalition partners. This operation was highly contentious, as Afghan farmers were resistant to replacing their lucrative poppy crops with **corn**—a policy widely regarded as a failure by those of us on the ground.

Later in my deployment, I was reassigned to the **Afghan Border Police Regional Training Center (RTC) in Gardez, Paktiya Province,** where I provided **mentorship and training assistance** to U.S. **State Department contractors** and Afghan Border Police trainees.

I returned to **Hawaii in August 2009,** and shortly after, my ex-wife and I agreed that our **13-year-old son, Jonathan,** should come to live with me. Recognizing the challenges of Hawaii's public high schools, I later made the decision to relocate him.

I also knew that my time and career in the Army were rapidly coming to a close. Being from Iowa, I knew that getting my son back to the Midwest, in a good school district, was my priority at that time. I found a vacancy at the Provost Marshal's Office (PMO) at Rock Island Arsenal, IL. Once I learned about the assignment, I knew it would be the best option for both Jonathan and me. In August 2010, I was assigned to PMO Army Sustainment Command at Rock Island Arsenal, IL. Jonathan was enrolled at

North Scott High School in Eldridge, Iowa, where we also found a home.

In the spring of 2011, I finally met the love of my life and my current wife, Traci Haxton.

We married on August 25, 2012, blending our families. Our home in Eldridge grew to five, as Trenton and Lauren from Traci's previous marriage became part of our family. Needless to say, the third time's a charm.

We have been married ever since, and we both know we found our soulmates. It hasn't been without challenges, but I wouldn't change it for the world. I thank God every day for her.

I retired from the Army in May 2013. Over the course of two decades, I attended numerous schools, including: Army Basic Training, Field Artillery Meteorologist School, Basic Airborne School, Army Combat Lifesaver School, NBC School, Primary Leadership Development Course (PLDC), Basic Military Police School, Air Movement Operations, Basic Non-Commissioned Officer Course (BNCOC), Advanced Airborne School (Jumpmaster School), Army Instructor Course, Advanced Non-Commissioned Officer Course (ANCOC), Conventional Physical Security Course, Basic and Advanced Anti-Terrorism Program Courses, Electronic Security Systems Course, and Security Operations Course.

After retiring from the Army, I completed my bachelor's degree in Criminal Justice from Upper Iowa University in 2013.

In January 2014, I was hired by and joined the Eldridge Police Department.

There, I served in the patrol division and as the department's primary firearms instructor. I conducted numerous criminal investigations and served arrest warrants. Additionally, I attended various training programs, including Firearms Instructor Course, Rifle Instructor Course, Field Training Officer Course, Glock Armorer's and LMT Defense Armorer Courses, Crisis Intervention Course, and the Reid Institute for Interviews and Interrogations Course, among others.

Serving the people of our community was one of the most rewarding aspects of my job. The people I encountered and the lives I touched made it all worthwhile.

I retired from the Eldridge Police Department in January 2023.

I later took a job with Hy-Vee, where I am currently employed as a Retail Security Officer.

Over the last three decades, I have served my city, state, and country in different capacities.

I have fulfilled this sense of duty not as an obligation but as a calling—to serve and give of myself for my community. Over the years, this service has come at a personal cost, including missed birthdays, holidays, parent-teacher conferences, and even divorces. However, I hope my loved ones understand that my service came from a deep sense of purpose that has been with me since childhood.

I also hope that this same sense of duty and selfless service is not lost on future generations in our great country.

BIBLE SCRIPTURE ON WHAT TO THINK ON

Philippians 4:8 (KJV)

"Finally, brethren, whatsoever things are true, whatsoever things are honest, whatsoever things are just, whatsoever things are pure, whatsoever things are lovely, whatsoever things are of good report; if there be any virtue, and if there be any praise, think on these things."

I'm not saying all police are perfect; I'm saying I choose to focus on the positive things I know and have heard about them.

PRAYER FOR POLICE AND FIRE FIGHTERS

Thank you, God, for the police and firefighters who sacrifice their lives on a regular basis, responding to dangerous situations.

They often have to leave their families for long hours, not knowing what they will face, while their loved ones wait, unsure if they will see them again.

Thank you, God, for the safety you provide through the police and firefighters. Help us to focus on those who do good and to pray for those who do not.

In Jesus' name, Amen.

1st African American female firefighter hired in the state of Iowa (1986–2014).

Thank you for your hard work and sacrifice!

www.ingramcontent.com/pod-product-compliance
Lightning Source LLC
Chambersburg PA
CBHW030846200726
48285CB00007B/2569